Domingo had a cat. It was a very fine cat. But apart from that, Domingo had very little else.

You see, Domingo was very poor indeed. As time went on, he had to sell more and more of his things in order to feed himself and his cat. Before long, he only had the cat left.

But Domingo was very fond of his cat.

“I will never part with you,” he said. “I will starve before I sell you.”

“You will never starve as long as you have me,” said the cat. “I will go out into the jungle and make our fortune!” And with that, the cat set off.

When he got to the jungle, the cat dug little holes in the earth. Every time he dug a hole, he found a silver coin. He took some of these coins home to Domingo to buy food with, and then he gave the rest to the King.

Domingo was very happy with the silver coins. That evening, he and his cat ate and drank like kings, and they slept like logs.

The next morning, the cat set off again into the jungle. This time, he dug up gold coins! As before, he gave some of the coins to Domingo, and the rest to the King.

The next morning, the cat went again to the jungle and set about digging his holes. This time, he found an emerald in every one. Again, he gave some to Domingo, and the rest to the King.

The King was very interested in the gifts, and where they came from.

He said to the cat, “Where do you get these expensive presents? Who is sending them to me?”

“Domingo sends them,” the cat replied.

The King thinks about what the cat has told him...

"This Domingo must be the richest man in the whole kingdom. I must marry him into the family..."

So he called for Fernanda, the oldest of his children.

"You must marry this man called Domingo," he said. "He is very rich!"

But when the cat told Domingo that he must marry Fernanda, he was shocked.

"I cannot get married in these rags," he said, pointing to his ragged coat. "And I have no fine house to bring my wife to when we are married."

“I will fix that,” said the cat. So he told the King that Domingo’s fine wedding coat had gone up in smoke.

“There was a fire at the tailor’s,” he lied.

The King gladly agreed to lend Domingo a fine coat for the wedding.

The next morning, the cat set off for the jungle again, this time with some scissors. He set about cutting down vines. When he had finished, he found an elegant house standing there in the jungle.

The house was marvelous! A wide river led up to it, and it had a big garden.

"This house will be perfect for Domingo and his wife," said the cat to himself.

So the wedding went ahead. Domingo looked very handsome in his fine coat, and Fernanda looked dazzling in her fine dress. And as Domingo and his bride sailed down the river to the fine house, they spotted the cat. He was singing for them in the garden.

But the next morning, Domingo's cat was nowhere to be seen. Domingo looked far and wide for him, but the cat had gone off into the jungle and was never seen again.

"Perhaps he has gone to make someone else rich," said Domingo to himself.